New York Times Best-Selling Authors
Henry Winkler & Lin Oliver

Here's HANK

URP!

Stop That Frog!

ILLUSTRATED BY SCOTT GARRETT

Grosset & Dunlap
An Imprint of Penguin Group (USA) LLC

There cannot be enough dedications to my incredible
partner, Lin Oliver, who is a creative surprise every day.
And to Stacey always—HW

For Carcake and Froggy, with hopes that life
in the puddle treated you well—LO

To Mum and Dad, for never telling me
to get a proper job!—SG

GROSSET & DUNLAP
Published by the Penguin Group
Penguin Group (USA) LLC, 375 Hudson Street, New York, New York 10014, USA

USA I Canada I UK I Ireland I Australia I New Zealand I India I South Africa I China

penguin.com
A Penguin Random House Company

Text copyright © 2014 by Henry Winkler and Lin Oliver Productions, Inc.
Illustrations copyright © 2014 by Scott Garrett. All rights reserved.
Published by Grosset & Dunlap, a division of Penguin Young Readers
Group, 345 Hudson Street, New York, New York, 10014.
GROSSET & DUNLAP is a trademark of Penguin
Group (USA) LLC. Printed in the USA.

Typeset in Dyslexie Font B.V.
Dyslexie Font B.V. was designed by Christian Boer.

Library of Congress Cataloging-in-Publication Data is available.

ISBN 978-0-448-48152-4 (pbk)   10 9 8 7 6 5 4 3 2 1
ISBN 978-0-448-48241-5 (hc)   10 9 8 7 6 5 4 3 2 1

The books in the Here's Hank series are designed using the font Dyslexie. A Dutch graphic designer and dyslexic, Christian Boer, developed the font specifically for dyslexic readers. It's designed to make letters more distinct from one another and to keep them tied down, so to speak, so that the readers are less likely to flip them in their minds. The letters in the font are also spaced wide apart to make reading them easier.

Dyslexie has characteristics that make it easier for people with dyslexia to distinguish (and not jumble, invert, or flip) individual letters, such as: heavier bottoms (b, d), larger than normal openings (c, e), and longer ascenders and descenders (f, h, p).

This fun-looking font will help all kids—not just those who are dyslexic— read faster, more easily, and with fewer errors. If you want to know more about the Dyslexie font, please visit the site www.dyslexiefont.com.

CHAPTER 1

"Today is a very special Wednesday," Ms. Flowers said to our class. "Can anyone tell me why?"

My hand shot up high in the air. "Because I changed my underpants this morning!" I shouted out proudly, without even waiting to be called on.

The whole class burst out laughing.

"As you can see, Hank," Ms. Flowers said, "we are all

very pleased for you. But your underpants are not exactly what I had in mind."

Before she could call on anyone else, our classroom door swung open, and Principal Love came in. He was carrying a tall glass tank with a bunch of leafy green plants at the bottom. As usual, he was wearing his Velcro sneakers, which squeaked when he walked in.

"Class, everyone say hello to Principal Love," Ms. Flowers said.

"Good morning, Principal Love," we all said at the same time.

"And don't forget to say good morning to Fred," he answered, pointing to the tank. "Fred's a little sleepyhead in the morning, aren't you, buddy?"

I squinted my eyes and looked at the tank. Who or what was Fred? Suddenly, a green blob with a pinkish belly and white spots on its back sprang out from behind a plastic log and attached itself to the side of the glass.

"There you are, you little froggy," Principal Love said. Then, turning to us, he added, "He wants to say hello because he's going to be a member of your class until next Monday."

"Does he know that we have a big spelling test this Friday?" my best friend Ashley Wong asked.

"Yeah, it's full of hard words like 'beautiful,'" my other best friend Frankie Townsend added.

"That's not a hard word for him," Principal Love said, "because he is such a beautiful frog."

"You call that thing beautiful?" Nick McKelty snickered. "It's all green and bumpy."

"Green is my favorite color,"

Katie Sperling said. "And besides, I think frogs are cute."

"I like to watch them suck bugs right out of the air and swallow them whole," Luke Whitman said. That didn't surprise me, because Luke likes everything gross. The grosser the better.

"Well, my pal Fred here likes to dine on crickets," Principal Love said. Reaching into his pocket, he pulled out a plastic container that had a whole bunch of crickets hopping around inside.

"Since I'm going to be away at a conference, Ms. Flowers has kindly agreed to have Fred stay in your classroom until I return. So I've brought him enough dinner to keep his tummy nice and full while I'm gone."

"Eeuuwww," Katie Sperling said. "I can't believe he wants to eat those gross things."

"He probably thinks cheeseburgers are gross," Ashley pointed out to her.

Everyone laughed. It was going to be fun to have a frog in our class. I especially liked having him there because it meant that I wasn't going to be the slowest reader anymore. I'm not very good at reading, but even I can read better than a frog.

"I promised Principal Love that we would all take very good care of Fred," Ms. Flowers said.

"He is my special pet, a White's tree frog," the principal explained. "I've had him for eight years."

"That makes him exactly our age," Frankie said.

"When's his birthday?" Ashley asked. "We could bake him cricket cupcakes."

"Yeah, with worm frosting," Luke Whitman added. "I'll eat one of those."

Principal Love was not amused. In fact, he seemed angry. The muscles in his face started to twitch, which made the mole on his cheek that looks like the Statue of Liberty without the torch seem like it was doing the hula.

"There is nothing funny about taking proper care of my prized frog," he said. "I trust that you will all give him the love and respect that he deserves."

"Oh, you can count on that, Principal Love," Ms. Flowers said. "You can go to your conference knowing that Fred is safe with us. Isn't that right, class?"

We all nodded so hard our heads almost rolled off our necks.

"Then I will see you all on Monday," Principal Love said. And turning to Fred, he said, "You be a good frog and remember the rules we discussed. No croaking during pop quizzes. No jumping on anyone's nose. And finish one cricket before you ask for seconds."

He put his hand on the glass, and Fred extended his front leg to meet Principal Love's fingers. I couldn't believe what I was seeing. They were shaking hands and saying good-bye.

Ms. Flowers walked Principal Love to the door. Then she carried Fred's tank over to the bookshelf that's under the window. She opened the blinds so Fred could look out on the playground and see the kids playing at recess. I don't actually know if frogs like handball, but I could tell that Fred had a very good view of the handball court.

We talked about all the things we would have to do to make Fred happy and comfortable in our class. Frankie volunteered to pick out frog-appropriate music and make a playlist for Fred. Ashley took on the responsibility of misting his tank with water, which kept the temperature froggy-comfortable. Luke wanted to chop up the crickets, but Ms. Flowers said that she thought Fred liked them whole.

"The last thing we have to decide," Ms. Flowers said, "is who gets to take Fred home over the weekend."

Everybody wanted that job. We all waved our hands in front of her face at the same time, saying, "Me! Me! Me!"

"Well, let's wait and see," Ms. Flowers said. "We'll observe Fred very carefully over the next few days. Maybe he'll give us a clue whom he'd like to go home with."

When the recess bell rang, everyone ran out of the classroom but me. I hung back and went over to Fred's tank. I pulled up Katie Sperling's desk chair and just watched Fred poking around in the leaves. I stared at him with all my might, and he stared back at me with his droopy, froggy eyes. I never took my eyes off him, and he never took his eyes off me.

Call me crazy, but I'll tell you this: I felt like I knew exactly what Fred was thinking.

CHAPTER 2

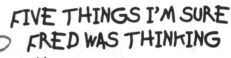

FIVE THINGS I'M SURE FRED WAS THINKING
BY HANK ZIPZER

1. I wonder how many kids in this class have peanut butter-and-jelly sandwiches for lunch.

2. This boy Hank is going to be my new best friend. I'm going to teach him how to croak.

3. Humans would be so much better-looking if they had green skin and bulging eyes.

4. What's with those chairs?
   I wonder why kids don't
   just sit on logs.
5. Why do you have to learn to
   spell, anyway? (Oops, that
   was me thinking, not the
   frog.)

CHAPTER 3

I don't want to brag, but of all the kids in our class, I'm sure Fred liked me best. When it was feeding time, three kids got to drop a live cricket into his tank. I didn't get a chance to feed him, but when I put my hand into his tank to change his water, he'd jump into my palm and sit there for a long time.

On Thursday, when I put my face next to the glass, he hopped out from underneath the leaves.

He jumped onto the glass next to my face and shot his tongue out, just like my dog, Cheerio, does when I come home from school.

On Friday, I took over the job of misting his tank with water. When I did it, he hopped off his log and let the drops of water fall down on him like a shower.

People don't usually think of frogs as cute. But I'm telling you this: Fred was the cutest.

Before lunch on Friday, Ms. Flowers told us it was time to pick who would get to take Fred home for the weekend. Katie Sperling raised her hand.

"I nominate Hank," she said. "Everybody can see how much

Fred likes him, and how well Hank takes care of him."

"That's because they both have webbed feet," Nick McKelty shouted out. "And slimy skin."

"Okay, that's enough, Nick," Ms. Flowers said. "Does anyone else have a nomination?"

"Yeah," McKelty called out. "I nominate myself."

Ms. Flowers wrote both our names on the board. "Boys, can you each tell us what would make Fred's visit to your house special?" Ms. Flowers asked.

"Yeah," McKelty said. "I'll teach that slimy frog to dance. I'll show him some of my awesome moves."

"Like tripping over your own big feet?" Katie Sperling said.

McKelty stuck his tongue out at her. It still had some of his yellow breakfast on it.

"Hank," Ms. Flowers said. "Your turn."

"Well, I don't know if I could teach Fred anything," I said. "But I sure would try to be his friend."

"Very good," Ms. Flowers said.

"Now can we take a vote?" Ashley asked.

Ms. Flowers hesitated for a minute, and I noticed she looked a little worried.

"Before we vote, I want to remind you what a big job it is to take care of another living thing," she said. "Especially when you are in charge twenty-four hours a day."

I could tell that Ms. Flowers was talking directly to me. I'm not always as responsible as I should be. I mean to do the right thing, but sometimes my brain takes a vacation and forgets.

"Hank, if you win, are you sure you want to take on this responsibility?" Ms. Flowers asked.

Frankie's hand shot up in the air. "Ashley and I live in the same apartment building as Hank," he said. "We will be right there if he needs any help."

"Thank you, Frankie," Ms. Flowers answered. "That's being a good friend. So . . . all in favor of having Hank take Fred home, raise your hand."

Every hand went up except one. I think you can guess who didn't vote for me. That's right. Nick McKelty. He only got one vote and that was his own.

Maybe next time he calls me a loser, he'll think about that!

When everyone else left for lunch, I stayed with Ms. Flowers to go over all the rules for taking Fred home. She called my mom at our deli, the Crunchy Pickle, and got her permission for Fred to spend the weekend with us. My mom even told her that my grandfather, Papa Pete, would come after school and bring one of our delivery carts from the deli so we could roll Fred's tank home.

"It may smell a little like pickles and pastrami," my mom said. "I hope the frog doesn't mind."

"Oh, he won't," I shouted into the phone. "Fred and I like the same things . . . except crickets. I'm not a fan of crunchy crickets."

I could hardly wait for school to end. When the bell rang and all the kids filed out of class, Nick McKelty hung around just long enough to make a final nasty comment.

"I bet you and the frog get married this weekend," he said. "You make a great couple."

I tried to come up with a clever answer, but before I could get one out, he was gone. Just like the bully he is, McKelty likes to say something stupid and then slink away.

Ms. Flowers put together a weekend bag for Fred. She put in his misting bottle, his container of live crickets, and a list of instructions. The first one she wrote in red to make sure I'd remember it.

"Make sure you ALWAYS replace the screen cover on top of the tank, so that Fred cannot jump out," it said.

"Hank, do I need to go over these instructions again with you?" she asked.

"No, Ms. Flowers," I answered with confidence. I knew all the rules, including how and when to feed Fred. "I've memorized them ten times," I told her.

Ms. Flowers helped Frankie, Ashley, and me carry Fred and his tank downstairs. Papa Pete was waiting at the front door with a metal pushcart from the deli. Wow, my mom wasn't kidding. You could smell the pickles a mile away.

"Nice to meet you, Fred," Papa Pete said as he carefully placed the tank on the cart. "Welcome to Zipzer World. We've got a big weekend planned for you. We'll start with a roller-coaster ride, then a visit to the circus, and finish up with a trip to the top of the Empire State Building."

"Really?" Ashley said.

"No, not really," I said with a laugh. "Papa Pete is always joking around."

"How about we start with a nice roll home," Papa Pete said. "I'll get you kids an ice-cream cone on the way. What flavor do you think Fred wants?"

"A double scoop of cricket,"
I said. "With fly sauce instead
of chocolate."

We all cracked up as we
headed down 78th Street toward
home. I felt so happy that I
wanted to hop, just like Fred. It
was going to be a great weekend.

CHAPTER 4

After we ate our ice cream, we headed right to our apartment. As we walked, I began to wonder whether Cheerio was going to like Fred. Then I started to worry about it.

"Do dogs and frogs get along?" I asked Papa Pete.

"It depends on which dog and which frog," he answered. "If you're talking about Cheerio, we'll just have to

wait and see how he reacts."

We walked into the living room and put Fred's tank down on the coffee table. Cheerio, who had been asleep, jumped off the couch and sniffed all around the tank. His little nose was working overtime, and his tail was wagging like crazy. And the strange thing was that Fred was not afraid of Cheerio. In fact, he came out from behind the plants in his tank and jumped onto the glass. His bulging little eyes opened wide and stared right into Cheerio's.

"Well, look at that," Papa Pete said. "It looks like they want to meet each other."

"Ms. Flowers said it was okay for us to take Fred out of the tank, as long as we keep our eyes on him," Frankie said.

"Hank, you should hold him," Ashley suggested, "since he likes you best."

Ashley carefully took the screen top off the tank, and I reached in to pick up Fred. He settled into my hand and never took his eyes off Cheerio.

Cheerio let out the sweetest little whimper and put his nose right on the top of Fred's head. Fred let out the funniest little croak you've ever heard. That scared Cheerio, who backed up on his short legs.

"It's okay, boy," I said to him. "Fred is just talking to you."

"I wonder what he's saying," Ashley said.

Before we even had a chance to guess, Fred leaped out of my hands and onto Cheerio's back. Cheerio waited until Fred was comfortable, then took off trotting around the apartment.

Fred looked all around, checking out the carpets and furniture legs, croaking happily.

"Now we know what Fred was saying," Ashley said as we all laughed. "He was saying, 'Hey, Cheerio, take me for a ride.'"

"In all my years," Papa Pete said, "I have never seen anything like this. It's amazing."

He took out his phone and snapped a picture of Cheerio and Fred.

"Wait until I show this to my bowling team," he said. "They're not going to believe it. I don't even believe it, and I'm watching it happen!"

We were so interested in Cheerio and Fred that we didn't even hear the front door open. It was my dad and my sister, Emily.

My dad was carrying a large bunch of red and pink roses.

"Hi, everyone," he called out. "Emily and I got your mom's favorite flowers for her birthday tomorrow. She's going to be so—"

He was interrupted by Cheerio, who bolted across the living room to say hello. Fred had to hang on with all four of his little legs. As Cheerio ran across the room, Fred looked like a rodeo star riding a bucking bronco.

I lunged for him and grabbed him off Cheerio's back just before he went flying into the air.

"What is that, and why is it here?" Emily asked, pointing to my hands.

"*It* is a *he*, and his name is Fred. He's my guest for the weekend."

"Have you gotten Katherine's permission for him to stay here?" she asked. Katherine is Emily's iguana, who doesn't have a friendly bone in her body. I could say the same thing about Emily, but I won't.

"I'm sure Katherine will be glad to have another reptile in the house," I told her.

"Frogs are amphibians, not reptiles," Emily said in her most know-it-all voice. "Reptiles have scales."

"Just like you," I said in my most funny voice.

"Hank, you and your sister are turning this house into the Zipzer zoo," my dad said. "Where is this frog going to stay? He can't stay on the coffee table. That's where I'm putting your mother's birthday flowers."

"He'll stay in Hotel Hank," I said. "Otherwise known as my room."

"Ashley and I will help you carry the tank in there," Frankie said. "Come on, Ash."

Frankie and Ashley picked
up the tank and headed to my
room. I said a quick good-bye to
Papa Pete, then followed them,
carrying Fred in my hands. We
all knew that we had to get out
of there fast, before my dad said
Fred couldn't stay. We placed
the tank on my desk, next to my
bed. Carefully, I put Fred down
on his plastic log, and Ashley put
the screen cover on tightly.

"I'm going to go fill up his dish with fresh water," I said. "You guys wait here."

"We can't," Ashley said. "It's time for dinner. We have to go."

"Okay. Then come over tomorrow morning, and we'll plan something fun for Fred for this weekend."

They headed for the door, and I headed for the bathroom sink. Before she left, Ashley turned to me and said, "Hank, don't forget. After you put Fred's dish in the tank, put the cover back on, so he can't get out."

"Of course I will," I told her. "I know that rule best of all."

They left, and I went into the

bathroom and filled Fred's dish
with nice cool water. After I put
it in his tank, I reached in and
gave him a little rub on the head.
He croaked as if to say, "That
feels good."

"Hank," my dad called from the
living room. "I need you in here
right away to sign your mother's
birthday card."

"In a minute, Dad," I called out.

"Not in a minute," he called
back. "Right now. We need to do
it before your mother gets home."

I turned to Fred.

"I'll be right back," I told him.
"Make yourself at home."

Then I hurried into the living
room. Dad was signing the card,

and Emily was busy wrapping
a present for Mom.

"Help me with this," she said.
"Put your finger on the ribbon
while I tie the bow."

It seemed to take her forever.
She kept tying and untying the
bow until she got it to look just
the way she wanted it.

"Hurry up, Emily," I said.

"What's the big rush?" she
asked.

"I have to get back to Fred."

"Why? He's safe inside his tank.
You put the top on, didn't you?"

"Of course I . . ."

Uh-oh. Did I? Or didn't I?

I pulled my finger off the ribbon
as fast as I could.

"Hank, you ruined my bow,"
Emily yelled.

But I didn't care. I was only
thinking about one thing . . . Fred.
I raced to my room as fast as
my legs could go, hoping that I'd
find him safe in his tank where
I had left him.

CHAPTER 5

As I pushed open the door to my room, my heart sank all the way down to my shoes. I could see the screen cover lying on my bed. It was definitely not where it was supposed to be. But maybe Fred was still in there.

I ran across the room to get a closer look. Everything in the tank was just as I had left it . . . except that Fred wasn't there. I pushed aside all the plants to see if he was hiding in

the leaves. He wasn't. I picked
up the hollow plastic log to see
if he had wiggled inside it. He
hadn't. He was just plain gone.

"Fred!" I called out, looking
desperately around my room.
"This isn't funny. Come on out
from wherever you're hiding."

There was no answer. Not
even the smallest croak.

I got on all fours and looked
under my bed and under my
desk. I even picked up my
wastebasket and looked in.
There was nothing there but a
plastic spoon with chunks of
last night's strawberry yogurt
crusted on it.

What had I done? Had I lost

Fred forever? What was wrong with me that I couldn't even follow the one most important rule? I knew that rule, I really did. I went over it and over it. But somehow, it just fell out of my brain.

I pounded my forehead with the palm of my hand, hoping to get my brain working again. That must have shaken something loose, because an idea suddenly popped into my head.

I crouched into my best frog position and tucked my legs up next to my chest. Then I started hopping around my room and croaking, trying to sound just like Fred. I hoped that I was saying something cool in frog talk. Something like, "See, we can have a lot of fun together. We can hop the night away, so come on out."

I hopped and croaked for what must have been five minutes. My legs and throat were getting really tired, but I couldn't give up. That frog was my responsibility, and I wasn't going to stop until I found him.

I did stop, though, when I

heard a hissing sound at my bedroom door. I looked up to see my sister, Emily, standing there, with Katherine draped around her shoulders like a scarf. Although Emily has been known to hiss, this time it was Katherine making the noise.

"Katherine is annoyed by your stupid frog imitation," Emily said.

"Tell your lizard I'm not stupid," I shot back.

"Then why are you acting stupid?"

"I really need to find Fred, and you're not helping the situation. He got out."

Emily glanced over at the tank and saw the screen cover lying on my bed.

"He didn't just *get* out," she said. "You *let* him get out. And you say you're not stupid? You didn't even put the cover back on."

"Emily, I don't need your comments right now. So just take your hissing friend and go. I've got to call Frankie. At least he's someone who's willing to help."

As Emily turned to go, Katherine looked at me and let out another hiss.

"And I don't appreciate your advice, either," I said to the iguana, just in case she could understand English.

I ran into the living room, picked up the phone, and called Frankie. It took me three times to get the number right. I know his phone number by heart, but in my mind, the numbers always get flipped around.

"Frankie," I said as soon as he answered. "I have a problem. Can you come here right away?"

"No can do, Hank. It's family game night. I'm stuck here."

"Then come tomorrow first thing. And bring Ashley. It's an emergency."

"What's the emergency?" a voice from behind me said. It was a voice I was hoping not to hear. The voice of my dad.

I hung up and turned to him, trying to smile in a real casual way.

"Oh, it's nothing important, Dad. Just kid stuff."

"Hank, don't lie to me. Your voice didn't sound like just kid stuff."

"Okay, fine. I'm in trouble. It's Fred—I've lost him."

My dad sighed. I'd heard that sigh a million times.

"It's always something with you, Hank. Your mom is on her way home now, and I've made her favorite Chinese chicken salad as a pre-birthday surprise. I'm not going to let you ruin this dinner with your missing frog."

"But, Dad . . . Fred is lost!"

"He's not lost, he's just misplaced. He has to be here in

the apartment somewhere. We'll find him after dinner. Now go wash up."

"What if Fred is in trouble? What if he jumped in the toilet bowl . . . or is stuck in my gym shoes and faints from the smell?"

"Hank. Go . . . wash . . . up. We will deal with this after dinner."

My mom came home and was so happy to see her birthday flowers and favorite meal. I was going to tell her about Fred, but my dad shot me a warning look that meant **NOT NOW.** Instead, we just sat down to dinner.

"Oh, Stanley, this chicken salad looks so delicious," she said. "Doesn't it, kids?"

I nodded yes but didn't mean it. As I looked down at my plate, I kept hoping I'd see a little frog face peeking out from behind the lettuce.

But all I saw was a chunk of chicken.

Oh, Fred . . . what have I done?

CHAPTER 6

After dinner, everyone in the family went on a hunt for Fred. We looked everywhere. And I mean everywhere.

A LIST OF THE PLACES WE LOOKED
BY HANK ZIPZER

1. In the cookie jar. I didn't find Fred, but I found six gingersnaps, which gave me the energy to keep going.

2. In my dad's sock drawer. No frog there, but I did find a nose-hair clipper. I closed that drawer really quickly.

3. In Katherine's cage, including under the newspapers at the bottom.

Do the words "iguana droppings" mean anything to you?

4. Under the pillows of the couch. He wasn't there, but I did find $1.36 in loose change.

5. On the terrace off our living room. I didn't see Fred, but I did get a great view of the red neon Harvey's Pizza sign at the end of our block. Boy, oh boy, did I ever want a slice of pepperoni. (I know which you're thinking. How could I eat with Fred missing? What can I say, except that worrying makes me hungry.)

In the end, we never found Fred that night. He had vanished without a trace.

CHAPTER 7

Frankie and Ashley arrived bright and early the next morning. I had already put out three pairs of my mom's rubber gloves on the dining-room table. Next to the gloves, I laid out the butterfly net that came with my Junior Science Explorer Kit. Next to that, I added a medium-size strainer that my mom uses for making some of her horrible vegetable dishes. And next to that, I placed the

plastic container that we use to
store leftover potato salad.

"What's going on?" Frankie
asked me, looking at the
assortment of things I had put out
on the table.

"Welcome to Fred's search-
and-rescue team," I answered.

"Where's the team?" Ashley
asked.

"We're it. And these are our
tools."

"A butterfly net?" Frankie
asked.

"Some people call it that.
I prefer to call it a Frog Scooper."

"And what's the strainer for?"
Ashley asked.

"I couldn't find another net.

So the plan is we wait until my mom and dad leave for the movies. The minute Emily gets picked up for her reptile show and Papa Pete arrives to watch us, we set out on our frog-finding mission."

"You actually think that Fred is somewhere out in the neighborhood?" Frankie asked.

"I was watching him when we walked home from school, Frankie. And I saw him looking at that puddle on 78th Street. The one in front of Mr. Park's grocery store. I'm pretty sure that's where he would go."

"Are you saying," Ashley asked, pushing her glasses up

on her nose, "that you think Fred took the elevator down to the street and hopped away?"

"Why not?" I answered. "He's got suction cups on his toes, so he could climb up to the elevator buttons with no problem."

"I guess anything's possible," Frankie said with a shrug.

We raced around gathering the rest of the supplies: granola bars in case we got hungry, a magnifying glass to look for frog footprints, and pad of paper to write down clues. As I bent down to look for a pen on the coffee table, I almost tripped over Cheerio.

"Hankster, what's that your crazy dog is doing?" Frankie asked.

Cheerio had picked up one of my mom's roses and was walking across the living room with it between his teeth.

"Hey, those are Mom's flowers," I said, taking the rose out of his mouth. "If Dad sees this, he's going to get mad at me."

"Why?" Ashley asked. "You didn't do anything. Cheerio did."

"Yeah, but he's my responsibility, just like Fred is . . . I mean . . . was."

Ashley took the rose from me and put it back in the vase.

"How come your dad only bought nine roses? That's weird. People usually buy a dozen."

"Oh, that's great," I said. "Now we have one missing frog and two missing roses."

"Make that three missing roses," Frankie said with a little smile. "Twelve take away three is nine."

"You know me and math," I said. "We're not exactly best buddies."

By the time my parents and Emily left and Papa Pete arrived, we had packed all our frog-finding equipment in a shopping bag, and had our jackets and rubber gloves on.

"What's this?" Papa Pete
asked when he saw us. "Are we
going on a science field trip?"

"We're on a mission," I told
him. "Fred is lost, and he could
be in terrible danger."

"Hank thinks Fred ran away to the puddle on Seventy-eighth Street," Frankie added.

"That's quite a theory," Papa Pete said. "We better go see if you're right."

That's what I love about my grandfather. He never makes fun of any of my ideas. And he's always willing to try anything. You can't say that about most grown-ups.

"Do I have time to grab a cheese Danish from the kitchen?" Papa Pete asked.

I shook my head. "We'll snack later. Frogs before food. That's our motto."

As we hurried out the door,

I noticed Cheerio walking over to the vase and taking another one of my mom's roses. I had no idea why he was suddenly so interested in flowers. Usually all he wants to do is pee on them. But I had no time to find out. I had to get Fred before anything horrible happened to him in that puddle.

We couldn't waste any more time. It took forever for the elevator to come. And once it did, it seemed like we would never get down to the lobby. When the doors finally opened, we raced outside.

"Here we come, Fred!" I shouted.

If only he could hear us . . .

CHAPTER 8

We ran all the way to the corner of 78th and Amsterdam Avenue. It's only half a block away, but it seemed like a hundred miles because I was so worried about Fred. When we got there, Mr. Park was outside his grocery store, putting water into the buckets that held all the flowers for sale. He looked at the three of us wearing rubber gloves and carrying our supplies.

"Are you going fishing?"
he asked with a laugh.

"No, Mr. Park," I answered
seriously. "We're going
frogging."

He looked puzzled.

"I've never heard of this
sport," he said.

"It's not a sport," Ashley
explained. "We're on a mission
to find a lost tree frog named
Fred."

"You didn't happen to see
him hopping by, did you?"
Frankie asked.

"I see many strange things
on this corner. I see dogs
wearing red boots. I see ladies

wearing the same boots. I see
children with shoes that light up.
But one thing I don't see is frogs."

Mr. Park went back to watering
his flowers, and we gathered
around the puddle to check it
out. The puddle had started out
pretty big, but it was getting
even bigger from Mr. Park's
watering hose. If we stepped
in it, it would probably come
up to our ankles.

"So what's your plan, frog
finders?" Papa Pete asked.

"First, we check it out with
our eyes," I said.

Frankie, Ashley, and I all
stared down into the puddle.

"Anybody see anything frog-
like?" I asked.

"Does a green leaf count?"
Frankie said.

"No."

"Then I don't see anything."

"So now we have to use our nets," Ashley said, pulling the strainer out of the shopping bag.

She put the strainer at the edge of the puddle and pulled it through the water. I could hear the metal scraping against the pavement.

"Look what I found!" she exclaimed.

"Is it Fred?" Frankie and I asked at the same time.

"No. A nickel."

Papa Pete laughed.

"This frog search pays well," he said. "Find another nickel and you can buy yourself a gumball."

Ashley continued to scrape her strainer around the edges of the puddle. She found a soggy candy wrapper, a gray pebble, and half a yellow crayon.

"If Fred is in here, I think he'd be in the deeper part of the puddle," I said. "In the middle. I'm going to use my net. It has a longer handle."

I took a step or two into the puddle.

"Don't get yourself wet, Hankie," Papa Pete warned.

"Don't worry," I told him. "I have my boots on."

I leaned over and held my net out as far as it would go. Out of the corner of my eye, I thought I saw something move. Could it be Fred? My heart

started to race, and I reached
out to dip my net into the
water.

WHOMP! Before I knew what
had happened, I was facedown in
the puddle.

When I looked up, I saw
a French poodle in a pink
sweater zooming by me. "What
happened?" I said.

"That little dog cut you off
at the knees," Frankie said,
laughing so hard he was almost
crying.

"Fifi!" a woman called. "Get
back here at once. Look what you
did to that nice young man."

Fifi zoomed by me again,
dashing through the puddle and
splashing me in the face. Now it
was Ashley's turn to laugh.

"I'm sorry, Hank," she said,
trying to control herself. "It's
just that you look so funny
sprawled out in that puddle."

"It's a good thing Fred isn't in there, or you would have crushed him," Frankie added.

Papa Pete reached his big, strong hand out to me.

"Let's get you out of there," he said. "You're soaked."

When I stood up, I was covered with puddle water.

"Look, there's hardly any water left on the pavement," Frankie said. "The puddle's all over you."

"Check your pockets for Fred," Ashley suggested. "Maybe he hopped in when you were swimming around down there."

"Listen, kids," Papa Pete said, putting his hand on my shoulder.

"I know you want to find that frog really badly. But I have to tell you, I don't think he's on the street. Hank, you have to face the fact that you may not find Fred."

"I can't, Papa Pete. I can't go back to school without Principal Love's frog. I have to think of some way to find him."

Papa Pete sighed.

"In my experience, I've found that a hot slice of pepperoni pizza makes the brain work better. Let's go to Harvey's and think this problem through."

I was shivering—partly because I was cold, but mostly because I was so scared. Papa Pete handed me his red sweatshirt. It was so big that it looked like I was wearing a bright red tent. I didn't care, though. I had frogs on the brain.

We walked down 78th, passing our apartment building. Our neighbor Mrs. Fink was just walking in the front door. She was carrying a shopping bag that said "Pets for U and Me" on the outside. Probably she had just gone there to buy food for her angelfish, Marsha. As I looked at the shopping bag, suddenly an idea popped out of my brain like a jack-in-the-box.

"Do you think they sell frogs at Pets for U and Me?" I asked Frankie.

"Hank . . . are you thinking
what I think you're thinking?"
he answered.

Oh yes, I sure was.

CHAPTER 9

I convinced everyone to change direction and head to the pet store. Even though Frankie and Ashley had their mouths watering for pizza, they understood that I needed to get to the pet store right away. When I have an idea, I need to fly into action that very minute. And I was hoping that this idea was the answer to my Fred-the-Frog problem.

"If you're thinking that you can replace Fred with another

frog, you're wrong," Ashley said as we walked quickly down the street. "Don't you think Principal Love knows his own frog?"

"Maybe Fred has an identical twin in the back who's been really missing his brother," I said. "That could happen."

"Yeah, when penguins wear soccer shorts," Frankie said, opening the front door to the store.

As you go into Pets for U and Me, instead of a bell ringing, you hear the sounds of jungle birds and monkeys. You feel like you're in a South American rain forest.

"Hi, how can I help you today?" George said, coming out from behind the cash register. "Did you come for some treats for Cheerio?"

It's cool that George knows all the animals in the neighborhood.

"I'm not here on dog business today," I told him. "I'm here on frog business. Please say you have a White's tree frog I can buy."

"Oh, they make great little pets," George said. "Let me check in the back and see what I have."

As George headed for his storeroom, Papa Pete put his hand on my shoulder.

"I like that you're trying to replace what you lost, Hank," he said. "But you cannot pretend that this new frog is the original."

While I was thinking about that, George came bouncing out, carrying a small plastic tub.

"It's your lucky day!" he said. "I've got just the guy for you."

We all looked inside, and there was a fat little frog, sitting on a green plastic log. He looked just like Fred!

"Can I hold him?" I asked.

"Sure," George said, scooping

the frog up. "Just hold him firmly in both hands."

The little frog sat comfortably in my palms. Suddenly, he made a noise that sounded just like a burp.

"Well, excuse you," George said to him. Then looking at me, he added, "He just had two crickets for lunch."

Frankie, Ashley, and I studied the little frog closely.

"He's about the same size as Fred," I said. "With the same little suction cups on his toes. And the same white spots on his back."

Ashley put her finger under his belly and gave him a little tickle. The frog moved, and my heart sank. His belly was not pinkish like Fred's. It was yellow. Definitely yellow.

"Do you happen to have one just like this but with a pink belly?" I asked George.

"I'm afraid this is the only one I have," George said. "I can be on the lookout for a pink-bellied one."

"I need it by Monday morning, before school," I told him.

"I'm sorry. I can't help you there,

Hank. You're sure this guy won't do?"

"He's a wonderful frog," I told George. "But no thank you."

We left the store and stood outside on the sidewalk. A cold breeze blew in our faces, reminding me that I was still soaking wet. I shivered.

"We better get you home and into some dry clothes," Papa Pete said. "I can always go pick up some pizza later."

"Thanks, anyway," I said to him. "I'm just not in the mood for pizza anymore."

What I had done was hitting me like a ton of elephants. I had lost Fred for good. And I was just going to have to face that.

CHAPTER 10

When we got to the apartment, I expected Cheerio to come running to say hello. But he was nowhere to be found.

"That's strange," I said out loud. "I wonder where Cheerio is."

"You just go change your wet clothes," Papa Pete told me. "He's probably asleep in his bed in the kitchen. I'll go look."

"Ashley and I will come with you," Frankie said. "Maybe there are cookies in there, too."

91

I walked into my bedroom and put on a pair of jeans that I had flung over the back of my desk chair. As I went to my bottom drawer to get out one of my many Mets sweatshirts, I noticed a strange thing. Actually two strange things. Just inside the drawer, where I had left it slightly open, were two red rose petals sitting on my gray sweatshirt. They floated to the rug as I pulled the sweatshirt out of the drawer. I wondered if my mom had put them there to make my drawer smell all rose-y. I would have to talk to her about that. I'd rather my drawers smell all baseball-y.

No one was there when I came back into the living room. I glanced at the vase on the coffee table. Was it my imagination, or did all the roses have fewer petals than before?

As I looked around the living room, I noticed that there were rose petals tucked all over the place. There were some under the coffee table. There was a little pile of them peeking out from behind the curtain. And a few were even half buried under the leather cushion of my dad's armchair.

"Hey, Frankie!" I called. "Hey, Ashley! Can you guys get in here right away?"

Frankie and Ashley came in from the kitchen, each one munching on one of my mom's flaxseed chocolate-chip cookies.

"These cookies aren't as bad as they look," Frankie said. "Here, we brought one for you."

"Thanks," I said, "but this is not cookie time. I've made what I think is an important discovery."

"Did you find Fred?" Ashley asked.

"No. But I found what I think is a clue."

I held my hand open and showed them some of the rose petals I had picked up from under the coffee table.

"I don't get it," Frankie said. "Your mom's roses are shedding. Why is that a clue?"

"Just watch," I whispered.

We stayed very still for a moment. Then, as we stood there, Cheerio came trotting into the living room through the doors from the terrace. He was too busy to even look up at us. Heading for the pile of rose petals tucked underneath the curtain, he picked a few of them up in his mouth, and went out the same way he had come in.

"Cheerio has scattered the
petals all over the house," I said.

"Your dog is going to get in
so much trouble from your dad,"
Ashley told me.

"There's got to be a reason,"
I said. "Let's follow that dog!"

I rushed over to the doors
that lead out to our terrace, with
Frankie and Ashley following close
behind.

We watched as Cheerio went to

one of the large clay planters that
holds my mom's favorite rubber tree.
He stood up on his back legs, his
front paws holding on to the edge
of the planter. Gently, he dropped
the petals into a hole in the dirt.
Then he whimpered gently, the way
he does whenever I rub his belly.

Except there was no belly
rubbing going on.

"Cheerio, are you doing what
I think you're doing, boy?" I
asked him.

And once again, without even looking up at me, he trotted right back into the living room.

We rushed over to the planter and looked down into the freshly dug hole.

"What do you see down there?" Frankie whispered right in my ear.

I was so excited, I could hardly speak. At the bottom of the hole was a pile of pink and red rose petals. And peeking out from under them was a pair of droopy eyes and a little froggy face.

"Fred!" I screamed. "I've found you! You're here!"

Ashley and Frankie leaned in to get a look into the hole.

"That's him!" Frankie yelled.

"Fred, we were so worried about you!" Ashley told him.

The three of us screamed so loud, we probably woke up the dinosaurs at the Museum of Natural History down the block! Papa Pete came running out to the terrace.

"You found him?" he cried. "Where was he?"

"In his new home in the planter," I explained.

Papa Pete looked confused. "His home in the planter?"

"Cheerio must have found Fred hopping around, and then tried to make a safe home for him," I reasoned. "That's probably why Cheerio scattered the petals all over the apartment."

"And then he found the perfect place to build a home— the planter," Frankie finished.

"That's wonderful, kids. Great detective work!" Papa Pete said. "Now let's hurry and put him back in his tank before we have to go on another search-and-rescue mission."

As I reached in to pick up Fred, Cheerio came running to the planter as fast as his little legs could go. He put himself right between me and Fred, and started to bark. It was as if he was saying to me, "Please don't take him. He's my friend."

I got down on one knee and reached out to pet Cheerio.

"I know how you feel, boy," I said gently to him. "I like Fred, too. But he belongs to somebody else. He can't stay here forever."

Cheerio put his head on my knee and let me scratch him behind his ears.

"We still have the rest of the weekend to enjoy Fred," I tried to explain to him.

"Yeah," Ashley said, bending down to join in our scratch fest. "Why don't you start by taking Fred for a ride on your back?"

"Whoa there, kids," Papa Pete said. "That frog has to go back in his tank."

"That's the idea," Frankie said. "Cheerio can be his taxi."

I reached into the dirt hole and gently lifted Fred out. Cheerio stared at his droopy little eyes,

and . . . I know this sounds
weird . . . but I'm sure he smiled.
Fred didn't smile back, but he did
blow up his throat to the size of
an English muffin and let out a
long, low croak.

Cheerio looked so proud when
I placed Fred on the middle of his
back.

"Okay, boy," I said to him.
"You're the driver. To my room,
please."

We all followed as Cheerio trotted happily into my room. When we got to the tank, Cheerio paused. Then he spun around in circles like he was chasing his tail. Fred hung on tight. I hoped he wasn't the kind of frog who got dizzy on roller coasters. I sure didn't want to have to clean up froggy barf after the day we'd had. Well, after any day.

I thanked Cheerio for giving Fred such a fun ride. Then I lifted Fred and put him back on the plastic log in his tank.

"Remember to put the cover on," Ashley said.

"Trust me, I will never

forget that again," I told her.

Papa Pete seemed very happy to have our frog adventure end.

"Let's celebrate with some milk and cookies in the kitchen," he suggested.

"Great idea," I said as I headed for the door.

"Uh, Hank?" Frankie said.

"The cover to the tank. The one you were never going to forget?"

"What about it?" I asked.

"You forgot it."

I looked down at my bed, and sure enough, there was the cover.

Welcome to Hank Zipzer's brain!

CHAPTER 11

FIVE FUN THINGS WE DID WITH FRED FOR THE REST OF THE WEEKEND

BY HANK ZIPZER

1. We made French toast for breakfast. Fred had a cricket instead, but we put some syrup on the cricket, too.

2. We put Fred in the Jacuzzi in Emily's dollhouse. He got so relaxed, he took a two-hour nap.

3. We let him float around the bathtub on the plastic aircraft carrier Frankie and I glued together from a kit. He took another nap.

4. We made popcorn and watched monster movies on TV. I guess Fred didn't like them much, because he took a nap.

5. We played Monopoly. Fred never moved his piece. That's because he was taking a nap.

CHAPTER 12

On Monday morning at breakfast, I asked my dad if Cheerio could walk with us to school.

"I'd rather he didn't," my dad said. "His habit of sniffing everything he walks by will make you late."

"But, Dad, this is his last day with Fred," I argued. "And I'm sure they need to say good-bye. Besides, I promised Fred he could have one last ride on Cheerio's back."

"Oh no," my dad said. "I have

to draw the line at that. There will be no doggy-back riding as long as I'm in charge."

I knew that tone of voice. And I knew that I'd never be able to change his mind.

"Okay," I agreed. "Cheerio comes, but Fred stays in his tank. That's a deal."

"If Cheerio goes, then Katherine goes, too," Emily said through a mouthful of scrambled eggs.

"That's too many animals," my dad said. "You should always have more people than animals on any walk."

"But Katherine will be lonely and feel left out," Emily said.

"She's a very sensitive iguana."

She turned to my mom and smiled sweetly at her, which is something you don't see often.

"Would you do me a favor?" she asked my mom. "Could you give Katherine a bath in the sink after we leave? She finds that very relaxing."

"Emily, I have to go to work," my mom told her.

"Besides, we're not running an iguana spa here," my dad added.

"Fine," Emily said. "Then I'll just set up her favorite book outside her tank, so she can spend the morning reading."

"News flash, Emily," I said. "Lizards can't read."

"Katherine can. Her favorite book is called *The Big Book of Flies*. I read it to her before she goes to sleep."

"Oh, so that's why she hisses all night," I said.

I hurried into my room before she could say anything else. This time, I checked to make sure the cover was tightly in place on Fred's tank. When I returned to the living room with the tank in hand, my dad had already put Cheerio on his leash.

It's a good thing that PS 87 is only a block from our apartment building. By the time we reached the front steps, that frog tank had become very heavy. Frankie and Ashley were waiting for us at the school entrance. They wanted to say good-bye to Fred, too. Not Emily, though. She just kissed Dad good-bye and bolted into the building. As she ran up the stairs, Principal Love came running down.

"Fred!" he yelled. "My little buddy! It's so good to see you!"

He put his face right up next to the tank. *Poor Fred,* I thought. He was getting a real up-close view of Principal Love's mole.

"How'd the weekend go?"
Principal Love asked me. "Did
this little rascal give you any
problems?"

"Not even one," I answered.

"Yeah," Frankie agreed. "Piece
of cake."

"You can say that again."
Ashley nodded. "Things couldn't
have gone any smoother."

We all stood there, nodding
our heads like bobblehead dolls.

"I am so pleased to hear that,"
Principal Love said. "I have to
admit, Hank, when I heard that
you were taking him home, I was
a little nervous. I think we both
know that you can be forgetful
from time to time. I worried that

perhaps you might leave the top off, and Fred would get out."

I burst out laughing, a little too loud and a little too hard. Frankie and Ashley joined in. We sounded like a pack of laughing hyenas.

"Leave the top off!" I howled. "You must be thinking of someone else!"

Principal Love bent down and took the tank from my hands.

"Hello there, buddy," he said to Fred. "Do you want to come inside with Daddy?"

Just as he turned to head up the stairs, Cheerio let out several loud good-bye barks. Principal Love turned around, and I got a good look at the tank. Fred had jumped onto the glass and was hanging on with his little suction cups, looking down at Cheerio.

"What's all this about?" Principal Love asked.

"They're just saying good-bye," I explained. "Fred and Cheerio became very good friends this weekend."

"A frog and a dog?" he said with a laugh.

"You never know where good friends can come from," I said.

"That's ridiculous!" Principal Love exclaimed.

"It isn't to Fred and Cheerio," Frankie told him.

"They had a lot of fun playing with their toys," Ashley added.

"Toys? What kind of toys could these two possibly share?"

"Oh, rose petals. Dirt. Aircraft carriers. Stuff like that," I said.

Principal Love looked confused,

and I don't blame him. You had
to be there to believe it.

"Well, in any case, I owe
you my thanks for taking care
of Fred and following the rules,"
Principal Love said. "He
obviously had a fine time."

"You know me," I answered.
"Following the rules is what I'm
best at."

Cheerio looked at me, and I
looked back at him.

"Don't you dare say a word,"
I whispered to him.

Principal Love turned and
headed happily up the stairs
toward his office. Frankie,
Ashley, and I gave one another
a big old high five. Even Cheerio

got in on the action and lifted
his paw.

Sometimes it's good to
share secrets with your friends.
Principal Love would never know
that it took a search-and-
rescue mission to find that frog!

CHAPTER 13

THREE THINGS I LEARNED FROM MY WEEKEND WITH FRED

BY HANK ZIPZER

1. When you use a strainer to catch a frog in a puddle, do not put it back in the kitchen drawer.

2. Wearing rubber gloves for longer than a minute makes your hands sweat.

3. Frogs jump higher than you think they can, especially when you're not looking. So keep the lid on the tank.

4. I repeat, keep the lid on the tank.

5. I'm just making sure that I mentioned this: keep the lid ON the tank.

I know that this list has more than three things on it. Sorry, but that's just the way my mind works.